Seven Spunky Monkeys

JACKIE FRENCH KOLLER

Illustrated by LYNN MUNSINGER

Harcourt, Inc.

Orlando Austin New York San Diego Toronto London

Requests for permission to make copies of any part of the work should be mailed to the following address:
Permissions Department, Harcourt, Inc., 6277 Sea Harbor Drive, Orlando, Florida 32887-6777.

www.HarcourtBooks.com

Library of Congress Cataloging-in-Publication Data
Koller, Jackie French.
Seven spunky monkeys/Jackie French Koller; illustrated by Lynn Munsinger.
p. cm.
Summary: One by one, seven monkeys who go out to have a good time
wind up falling in love over the course of a week.
[1. Monkeys—Fiction. 2. Days—Fiction. 3. Counting. 4. Stories in rhyme.
I. Munsinger, Lynn, ill. II. Title.
PZ8.3.K834Se 2005
[E]—dc22   2004005757
ISBN 0-15-202519-7

First edition
H G F E D C B A

Manufactured in China

The illustrations in this book were done in
pen-and-ink and watercolor on Winsor Newton paper.
The text type was set in P22 Garamouche.
Color separations by Colourscan Co. Pte. Ltd., Singapore
Manufactured by South China Printing Company, Ltd., China
This book was printed on totally chlorine-free Stora Enso Matte paper.
Production supervision by Pascha Gerlinger
Designed by Lydia D'moch

Pic
J
Koller
main

For Sawyer, our own spunky minimonkey,
with love from Nana
— J. F. K.

For ten spunky cousins:
Kelly, Carol, James, Brandy,
Krissy, Allie, Jack, Alex,
Kendall, and Lara
— L. M.

Seven spunky monkeys
went on Sunday to the park,
to swing from trees,
play hide-and-seek,
and romp till after dark.

"How ape-solutely awesome,"
the seven friends remarked,
"to be a spunky monkey
on a Sunday in the park!"

They came upon a magic show
and stopped to get some kicks,
watching the magician
do some magic monkey tricks.

The beautiful assistant smiled
and blew a little kiss...
and when the monkeys left,
instead of seven, there were six.

Six spunky monkeys
went on Monday to the beach,
to frolic in the ocean blue
and run and jump and screech.

"We're wild and free and funky,"
the spunky six declared.
"No nasty little lovebug's
going to catch US unaware!"

They climbed into their monk' mobile
and took a little drive,
then stopped to do some dancing
at their favorite monkey dive.

MONK'S CAFÉ

FREE JAZZ

WELCOME to MONKS!

MONK 1

A swinging saxophonist
was a-dishin' up some jive . . .

and when the monkeys drove away,
the six were only five.

Five spunky monkeys
went on Tuesday to the zoo,
to aggravate the elephants
and tease the kangaroos.

"Ooo-wee! What fun we're having!"
the five cried out with glee.
"Bet those lovesick monkeys
wish they still were wild and free!"

They heckled a hyena
and chased a wild boar,
then stopped to buy some gumdrops
at Miss Monkey's candy store.

Miss Monkey was more charming
than she'd ever been before . . .

and when the friends went on their way,
the five were only four.

Four spunky monkeys
went on Wednesday to the fair,
to ride the roller coaster
and wrestle with the bear.

"We're very generous monkeys,"
they said with some chagrin.
"What other spunky monkeys
would have let that poor bear win?"

They stopped to get some Band-Aids
at the fair infirmary,
and ask if Dr. Monkey
could inspect an injured knee.

The doctor was so gentle,
just as kind as she could be ...
and when the monkeys headed home,
the four were only three.

Three spunky monkeys
went on Thursday to the gym,
to do their weekly workout
and limber up their limbs.

"Who needs those silly simians?"
the final three declared.
"We're just lucky we're the ones
that Cupid's bow has spared."

They strutted through the weight room
and posed beside the pool,
where a handsome bodybuilder
was instructing swimming school.

He made such an impression
in his bathing suit of blue...

that when the monkeys left the gym,
the three were only two.

Two spunky monkeys
went on Friday to the school,
to ridicule the rugby team
and call the coach a fool.

They couldn't help but wonder
why their friends passed up such sport,
for mushy talk and moonlit walks
and nonsense of that sort.

"Not you and me!" they shouted
as they charged in for some fun.
But THEY felt like the rugby ball
before the game was done.

Mam'selle Masseuse's gentle hands
were soothing as the sun . . .

and by that night the monkey count
was down to only one.

One spunky monkey
stayed home Saturday alone.
He sighed deep sighs
and rolled his eyes
and waited by the phone.

"This is dumb," he finally said.
"This monkey's going out!
 I'll show those lovestruck loser chimps
 what fun is all about."

He went down to the theater,
but the movie had begun,
so he went into the bakery
to get himself a bun.

The baker sweetly asked if he'd like
plain or cinnamon ...

BANANA
BREAD

PIES
CAKES
COOKIES

FRESH
DOughnuts

and then the spunky monkey count
was absolutely none.

Seven spunky monkeys
went one Sunday to the park,
to swing from trees,
play hide-and-seek,
and romp till after dark.

With seven spunky spouses,
the apples of their eyes,
and seven busy babies
who, it comes as no surprise,
were very, VERY spunky
for their minimonkey size.

"How ape-solutely awesome,"
the seven friends remarked,
"to spend a spunky Sunday
with our families in the park!"